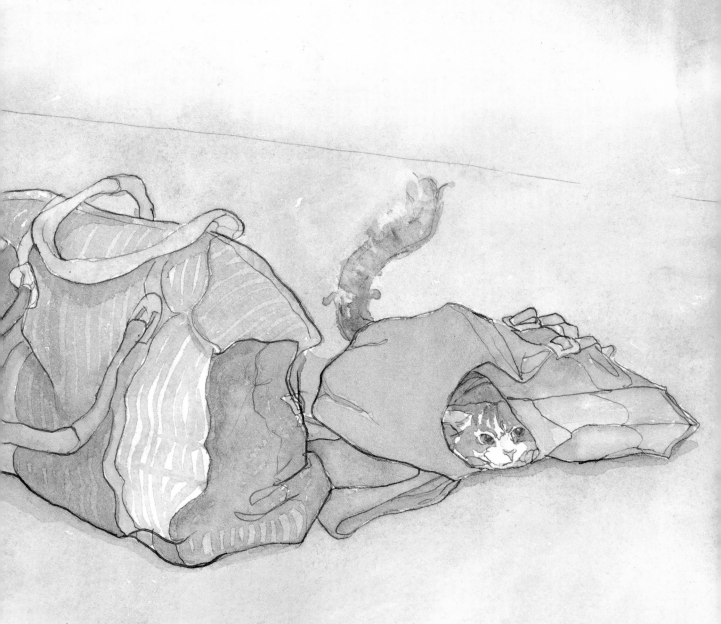

Pour ma mere.—J.O.

For my grandmothers, Eugena Pierce and Rosalina Santini. Prov. 22:6—D.S.

Text copyright © 1992, Jay O'Callahan
Illustrations copyright © 1992, Debrah Santini
Published by Picture Book Studio, Saxonville, MA.
Distributed in the United States by Simon & Schuster.
Distributed in Canada by Vanwell Publishing, St. Catharines, Ontario.
All rights reserved.
Printed in Hong Kong.
10 9 8 7 6 5 4 3 2 1

Library of Congress Cataloging in Publication Data
O'Callahan, Jay.
Tulips / by Jay O'Callahan ; illustrated by Debrah Santini.
p. cm.
Summary: Famous for his pranks, Pierre has never dared to play a trick on his Grand Ma Mere,
whose tulips grace one of the loveliest gardens in Paris; but one day, Pierre does dare.
ISBN 0-88708-223-8 : $14.95 [l.Grandmothers—Fiction.] I.Santini, Debrah, ill. II. Title.
PZ7.0164Tu   1992
[E]—dc20   91-41704
AC

Ask your bookseller for these other Picture Book Studio books
illustrated by Debrah Santini:
The Baby Who Would Not Come Down by Joan Knight
Santa's Secret Helper by Andrew Clements

Jay
O'Callahan

TULIPS

Debrah
Santini

Picture Book Studio

Someone had dropped the cat onto old Regis sleeping in his bed by the stove.

When Grand Ma Mere stepped into the kitchen, she saw everything with one sweeping glance. Then she announced, "Pierre has arrived."

But the kitchen servants had already figured that out.

In the whole world, Grand Ma Mere loved two things best: Pierre, and her wonderful tulips.

Everyone could see why she loved the tulips, for her garden was one of the largest and most beautiful in all of Paris.

As for Pierre...well, Pierre loved to play tricks.

Simple or complicated, sudden or slow, quiet or loud, Pierre loved tricks.

The whole household shuddered and cringed twice each year, for as surely as tulips must be planted in the autumn, and as surely as they bloom in April, Pierre came to Paris every fall and every spring to visit his Grand Ma Mere.

On the first morning of every springtime visit, Pierre and his Grand Ma Mere ate breakfast next to the curtained windows overlooking the garden.

"May we open the curtains now?" begged Pierre.

Grand Ma Mere acted as if she had not heard him, and asked, "Was your train ride pleasant, Pierre?"

"Oh yes, and I found the perfect trick to play on a train trip. I waited until all the passengers were asleep, and then I switched around all the tickets they had left out for the conductor to punch. When they woke up there was wonderful shouting and lots and lots of confusion...
it was a very good trick."

Grand Ma Mere's eyebrows went up and up and up.

Pierre reached for his fourth croissant, and his elbow knocked a teacup off the table. Somehow Grand Ma Mere caught it.

"How did you do that ?!" said Pierre.

"I watch things, young man. Now, wipe the jam off your mouth, and then you may open the curtains."

As Pierre pulled back the curtain, a servant threw open the French doors onto the terrace, and there they were: four hundred red tulips blazing in the morning sun.

Pierre gasped and ran to the railing, his eyes trying to see every flower all at once. It was a miracle every spring. Those little brown lumps that he helped to plant in the fall always turned into this amazing sea of red, red, red.

"Oh Grand Ma Mere! I think this is the best bunch ever!" said Pierre.

Grand Ma Mere was about to reply, but there was a huge crash behind them. The servant who had stood next to Pierre's chair during breakfast had dropped a tray of dishes.

Somehow his shoelaces had gotten tied together.

During the next five days, Pierre was busy.

The butler lost his keys, and did not find them until he had almost finished his oatmeal.

The gardener pulled on his boots and discovered a toad in one and a frog in the other.

The chambermaid looked
out the window one
afternoon to see her
bloomers hanging
from the flagpole.

And the buttons on
the servingmen's clothes
kept popping off at very
inconvenient moments.

On the day he left, Pierre thought he saw a little tear in the corner of Grand Ma Mere's eye, and she sighed as she kissed him goodbye.

The servants also came out to say goodbye, and as Pierre climbed into the back seat of the station car, they sighed too—but theirs was a great sigh of relief.

Over the summer, Pierre decided it was time to play a trick on his Grand Ma Mere. He thought and thought, and finally, after a visit to the garden shop near his home, he was ready for his grandest trick ever.

When he arrived at Grand Ma Mere's for his fall visit, Pierre had something special hidden in his suitcase, and the valet was surprised when Pierre said he would unpack his own things.

Very early one morning near the end of his visit, he crept out of the house and planted one more tulip bulb right in the middle of the great flower bed by the terrace. When spring came, one black tulip would bloom among all the red ones.

At breakfast, Grand Ma Mere said, "Pierre, you have muddy shoes."

"Yes, Grand Ma Mere, I went for a walk before breakfast."

Her eyebrows went up and up and up. "I see,"said Grand Ma Mere.

She was about to say something more, when there was a scream from the kitchen. It seems that a little snake had gotten into the sugar bowl.

Pierre chuckled to himself all winter
long, and when spring finally came, he
could hardly wait to go and visit Grand Ma
Mere for the opening of the tulips. He was so
excited that he forgot to play any tricks on the
train, and when he arrived at the great house in
Paris, he went straight to bed so he would be ready
for the morning.

At breakfast beside the closed curtains, Pierre said, "Grand Ma Mere, don't you just love surprises? Don't you think it's fun when things happen that are really unexpected?"

Grand Ma Mere said, "No, Pierre, I do not like surprises, and they never happen to me."

"But wouldn't you be surprised if one spring all the tulips weren't the same?" asked Pierre.

"Yes, but it will never happen. My gardeners and I are much too careful, and we choose our tulip bulbs with great care. They are always the same."

"I bet you that this year they are not all the same, Grand Ma Mere." And Pierre slipped one gold coin onto the table.

Grand Ma Mere's eyebrows went up and up and up.

"I disapprove of wagers, Pierre...but just this once, you have a bet."

Pierre jumped to his feet and pulled open the curtain.

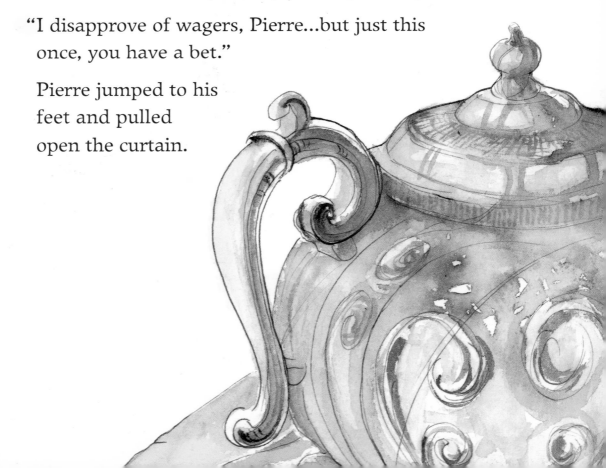

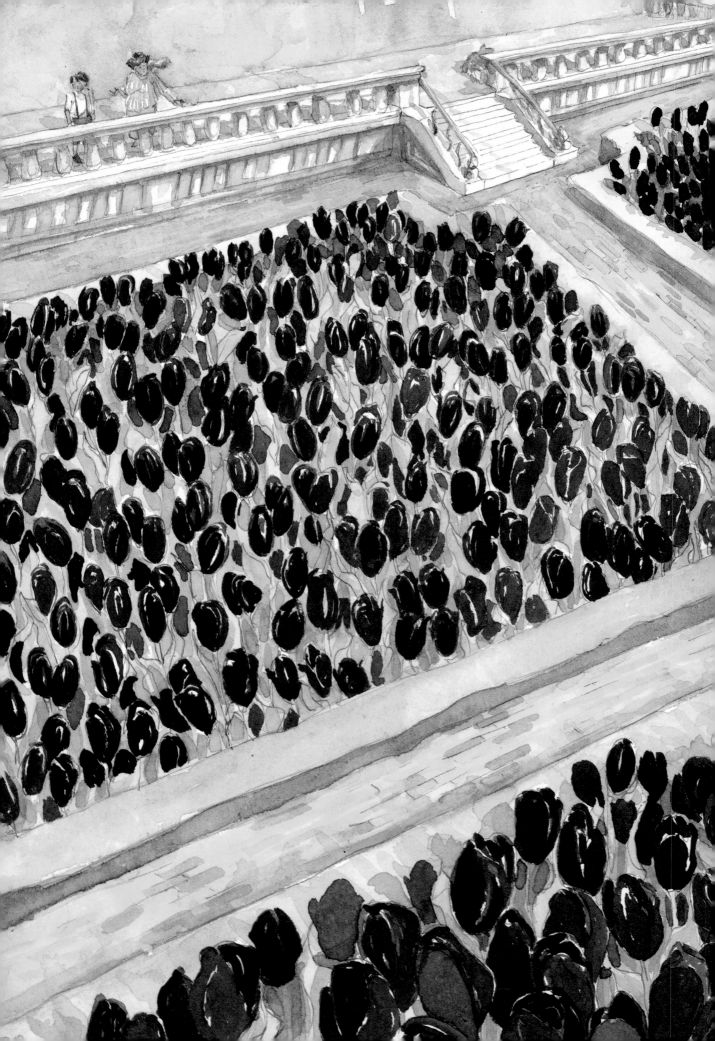

Pierre ran to the edge of the terrace and stared, his mouth wide open. Every single tulip was black.

Grand Ma Mere came and stood next to him.

Don't you think that black tulips make a refreshing change Pierre?" Then she held out her hand. "My gold coin, please."

As Pierre handed her the coin, he was almost sure that she winked at him.

When Pierre woke up the next morning, there was
a grasshopper in his sock (from the gardener),
some flour on his hair brush (from the cook),
a wet sponge in his shoe (from the butler),
a golfball in his cocoa (from the servingmen),
and a lump of soap on his muffin (from the chambermaid).

And under his pillow was one gold coin from his very
grand, very clever Grand Ma Mere.